WHERE STORIES MEET

Finding Courage, Community, and Calling in an
Imperfect World

A Novel with Devotional Elements

Grace Ajayi

Scripture quotations are taken from the Holy Bible, New International Version, NIV.

For more information or to contact the author, Email: gracetopublish@gmail.com

ISBN: 979-8-9939200-0-9 (paperback)
ISBN: 979-8-9939200-1-6 (ebook)

Cover design by Grace Ajayi
Interior formatting by Nathan Book Publisher Company

CONTENTS

✦ AUTHOR'S INTRODUCTION

"Every life tells a story, but sometimes it takes grace to help us hear our own."

Every life is a story, and some stories are quietly unfolding, waiting for a catalyst to reveal their profound beauty. I wrote this book because I believe that authentic faith isn't found in polished perfection but in the messy, courageous act of showing up imperfectly and vulnerably.

In a small church called Grace Commons, you're about to meet a group of down-to-earth, yet extraordinary and conventional people whose lives are about to become surprisingly and unexpectedly connected. They grapple with the same fears, doubts, and longings that resonate in our hearts: the struggle to belong, the terror of sharing one's true self, the weight of past mistakes, the hurt of unfulfilled dreams, and the quiet question of whether a seemingly small life can truly matter.

The book isn't a collection of long, perfect stories of faith. Instead, it's an invitation to see how a community based on grace can change lives, where "God doesn't need perfect, just available." As you read, I hope that you'll recognize parts of your journey, be inspired to do small acts of courage, and realize that God is waiting to use your story, with all of its beautiful flaws.

The result is a book about the quiet revolution that happens when we dare to be real, when we trust each other with our broken pieces, and when we finally understand that our greatest ministry often springs from our deepest wounds. May these stories inspire you to find your place in the unfolding narrative of grace.

Author's Note

This book is a mix of stories and spiritual thought. Each chapter ends with a story from someone's everyday life, along with questions and Scripture to help you think about what you've read, pray about it, and put it into practice. Think of the devotionals as a conversation with God. Write things down, be honest, and use what you learn during the week.

⬦ PROLOGUE

The Hum of Grace

Pastor Evelyn Ross often thought of Grace Commons not as a building, but as a living organism, always breathing, constantly changing. Fifteen years ago, when she'd first stepped into the role of senior pastor, she'd had a clear vision: to create a place where honesty was prioritized over perfection, where questions were welcomed more than easy answers, and where God's love wasn't diminished by human disappointment.

She knew the discomfort of feeling like an outsider, of carrying burdens unspoken. She'd seen too many people leave churches because they thought they had to pretend, to perform, to have it all together. But Evelyn believed God met people precisely in their unraveling. "God doesn't need perfect," she often said, "just available. He doesn't ask for wholeness, only for the courage to show up with your broken pieces." This philosophy had become the silent hum beneath the surface of Grace Commons, attracting souls who were tired of hiding.

Tonight, a Thursday evening in early fall, the prayer room would host another gathering. The scent of vanilla candles mingled with the quiet strum of a guitar, creating an atmosphere of gentle invitation. Evelyn looked around the semicircle of empty chairs, each one a potential haven for a weary soul. She thought of the wooden prayer box, its surface worn smooth by countless hands depositing whispered hopes and fears.

It wasn't about lightning bolts of clarity, she reflected. It was about the slow, steady work of grace, the kind that binds disparate stories together, finding purpose in unexpected places, and proving that sometimes, the most profound transformations begin with a single, trembling step into the light. These were the stories Grace Commons was built for, the quiet miracles she lived to witness. And tonight, another one was about to begin.

ACKNOWLEDGMENTS

Writing Where Stories Meet has been one of the most meaningful creative journeys of my life, and I am deeply grateful for everyone who has walked with me along the way.

First, I give all glory and honor to my Lord and Savior, Jesus Christ, my God, the Master Storyteller, whose grace continues to shape my life and whose presence inspired every page of this book. Without His strength, wisdom, and gentle reminders of purpose, this work would not exist.

I am deeply grateful to my husband, Olugbenga Ajayi, and our four beautiful daughters, Celine, Courtney, Charysse, and Christine. Thank you for your unfailing love, patience, and laughter. You are my constant source of joy, strength, and grounding. Your support made room for my creativity, and your belief in me helped bring this vision to life. Each of you inspires me in your own unique way, and I am grateful beyond words for the light you bring into my life.

To my spiritual family at church, thank you for your prayers, encouragement, and the environment of love and authenticity that continually fuels my passion for ministry. Serving alongside you has enriched my faith in ways words cannot fully capture.

I extend my heartfelt gratitude to the women in technology, emerging leaders, and faith-driven professionals. I mentor: you inspire me with your courage, resilience, and hunger for purpose. Though this book is fictional, your journeys remind me daily how powerful our stories can be.

To my dear Pastors, Pastor Ebenezer Ropo-Tusin and Pastor Olayide Ropo-Tusin, and to my beloved sisters Rita Omonoh, Mary Ajayi, Sandra Tomoloju, Maureen Chiekwe, Mosunmola Giwa, and Dr. Gloria Wright.

Thank you for your unwavering support, your constant push, and your ability to see greatness in me even when I could not see it myself. Your encouragement continues to strengthen me, especially throughout this journey, and I cherish each of you deeply.

To my friends near and far, thank you for celebrating every milestone, cheering through every late-night writing session, and reminding me that community makes the journey meaningful. Finally, to every reader holding this book, thank you. Thank you for opening your heart, embracing imperfection, and allowing these stories to speak to you. I hope that you find yourself somewhere within these pages and discover that God meets us right where our stories unfold.

With gratitude,

Grace Ajayi

1

WHISPERED IN THE PRAYER ROOM

Where Heaven Leans Close to Listen

Jeremiah 29:13 (NIV)
"You will seek me and find me when you seek me with all your heart."

Eli Thompson had never liked prayer meetings. They always seemed to be brimming with anticipation, which he hardly ever felt he could live up to. In a room full of people praying out loud, hands lifted, tears flowing, Eli always felt like an outsider. He felt as if he were holding a radio tuned to the wrong frequency. Still, he showed up. Reluctantly, he accepted his cousin Leah's invitation after she repeatedly nudged him. "Just come. It's not about being spiritual. It's about being real," she had said. At twenty-eight, Eli had grown tired of disappointing people, but he was even more tired of disappointing God. If God was still listening after two years of silence on Eli's part.

So, he was at Grace Commons Church at this very moment. An evening on a Thursday. There are low lights that cast warm shadows across walls that are cream colored. Soft acoustic guitar drifted from hidden speakers, mixing with the faint scent of vanilla candles and old hymnal pages. Eli's worn sneakers squeaked softly against polished hardwood as he made his way to a folding chair near the back. The chairs were arranged in a semi-circle with small tables to the sides holding pens, blank index cards, and a wooden prayer box that looked hand-carved, its surface worn smooth by countless hands. Eli settled into his seat, the metal cold against his back through his thin sweatshirt, where he hoped no one would notice him.

Eli never expected much that day. He slipped into the back seat, just out of view, hoping to blend in with the shadows. It felt safer that way. He felt undisturbed, unnoticed, and free from the weight of everyone's expectations. After all, he had already done what was expected of him. His cousin Leah had nudged him, almost with a soft urgency, to attend the meeting of the Saints. And he, dutifully, had come.

However, Eli had reconciled with the notion that he wasn't suited for this gathering and this place. It was a world that seemed to pass him by, and no matter how many prayers he whispered or how much he yearned for answers, God had grown silent on his case. So, in the midst of the gathering, where voices were lifted in praise and hope, Eli quietly told himself that the best way to honor this moment was simply to remain invisible.

After all, what else could he do when the silence of heaven seemed to speak louder than any sermon?

He scanned the room. Women in pairs muttering prayers, their voices creating a gentle murmur that reminded him of his grandmother's rosary prayers. An older man with weathered hands was already scribbling something on a card, and his peaceful face contrasted with the deep lines that indicated he had carried many burdens.

Every person who came in was greeted by Pastor Evelyn Ross, who stood at the front and shook their hand in a way that showed she saw them. "Welcome," she said, her voice soft but steady, carrying easily through the intimate space.

"Tonight isn't about perfection. It's about honesty. If you've come heavy, uncertain, worn out, or skeptical, you're in the right place."

Eli exhaled slowly, his shoulders dropping for the first time in days. He hadn't realized he'd been holding his breath, or maybe he'd been holding it for months. The air felt different now, thinner and almost as if he were exhaling the weight of his despair. It had been a long time since he'd felt anything special except a gnawing emptiness that clung to him like a second skin from his past experience.

It all began with the layoff. He remembered that day too clearly, as if it were inscribed into the very fabric of his bones. One moment, he was sitting in his cubicle, eyes glued to the screen, typing out emails like it was any other Tuesday. The next, he was walking out of that office with a box of his belongings in his hands, the weight of his future uncertain and hanging over him like a dark cloud. He'd been loyal. He'd worked his butt off, put in the hours, and stayed late when it counted. But loyalty meant nothing when the numbers didn't add up. And just like that, he was a casualty of corporate greed, cast aside like a piece of trash, no longer needed, no longer wanted.

It wasn't just the blow to his pride or his sense of self-worth. It was what came after the suffocating silence.

Where was God in all of this? He'd prayed for stability, guidance, and strength to get through each day. Instead, there was only an empty void where the answers should have been. He asked over and over, Why me? Why had this happened? Hadn't he been faithful? Hadn't he done everything right? But the silence? It was crushing. His prayers felt like they were bouncing off the walls, never reaching anything, never touching the heavens.

And then there was Sarah. His heart still twisted when he thought of her. He hadn't seen it coming and didn't expect the fracture in their relationship to be so deep, so swift. They'd built a life together, so he thought. A home and a future. But somewhere, somehow, it all unraveled. He hadn't noticed the signs until it was too late. One day, she packed her things, the goodbye falling from her lips like an afterthought.

Her absence created a hole in his life; it was a gaping void that swallowed everything in its wake. She wasn't just his partner; she had been his confidante, his anchor in the storm. And now, she was gone. And with her, it felt like his faith had slipped through his fingers, like sand slipping through a clenched fist. He'd prayed, begged even, for things to work out, for the love they once shared to reignite. But each night, he'd lay in an empty bed, staring at the ceiling, wondering if God had simply forgotten about him.

And maybe that was the real wound, the real struggle he couldn't shake, believing that God had forsaken him. Maybe he wasn't chosen like everyone else. Maybe God's plan didn't include him, or maybe, just maybe, he wasn't worthy of it. What had he done wrong? Where had he missed the mark? Each unanswered prayer seemed to confirm it: God had decided he wasn't enough. The plan for his life was still unfolding, but it wasn't unfolding the way he'd imagined, the way he'd hoped. It was like a book with pages torn out, leaving only fragments of a story he couldn't understand.

His faith had been shaken so violently that now, even the idea of stepping back into a church, lifting his hands in worship, or praying with any expectation felt like a cruel joke. What was the point when God seemed silent, distant, and far removed from his pain? Maybe he wasn't the one God cared about anymore. Perhaps he had just become one of the forgotten. All were the thoughts that roamed in his mind while Pastor Evelyn continued.

"At any point, you can write a prayer and drop it in the box. You do not need to include names or explanations; it is just between you and God. Sometimes the most powerful prayer is the one you don't say out loud." People began to move with quiet purpose. Some went toward the prayer box—some toward the front, where Pastor Evelyn waited with open arms. Eli stayed still, watching, his hands fidgeting with the frayed edge of his sweatshirt sleeve.

He was at a loss for words, even if he desired to write. His mind churned with the same questions that had kept him awake for weeks. Was God even listening? Had he ever been? What if he asked for something and nothing changed? What if something did, and he wasn't ready? What if God's plan was just as disappointing as everyone else's expectations? He pulled the hood of his sweatshirt up over his head, not because he was cold but because it made him feel invisible. The way he'd felt at the unemployment office. The way he'd felt when Sarah said she couldn't wait any longer for him to "figure things out."

A soft voice startled him from his spiral. "Thinking of leaving?" Eli turned. He was joined by a middle-aged man with salt-and-pepper hair and kind eyes. It was the same man who had been writing earlier. He wore a navy jacket that looked expensive yet comfortable, holding a pen in one hand and a folded card in the other. Something about his presence felt steady, like he'd weathered his storms and come out stronger. "No judgment," the man added, noticing Eli's defensive posture. "Just... you look like you're deciding something important."

"I guess I am," Eli said, his voice strained from disuse. "Want to talk about it?" Eli shrugged and then said, "I don't really engage in this kind of thing." The whole prayer thing. "I used to engage in this kind of thing," he said, stopping and surprised by his honesty. The man nodded with understanding. "Most of us don't. Until we have to. Until life gets so loud that we need somewhere quiet to put the noise." They sat in comfortable silence for a moment, the guitar music wrapping around them like a gentle embrace. "My name's Elias," the man offered.

"Eli." Elias chuckled, a warm sound that reminded Eli of his grandfather's laugh. "Look at that. "Perhaps God planned this seat." Eli cracked a smile, the first genuine one in weeks. "Maybe." Elias stood slowly, his movements deliberate. "When you're ready, just write what you wish you could say out loud. It's not for them," he gestured toward the room. "It's for Him. And He's got patience for broken sentences and messy handwriting." Then he walked away with quiet dignity, placing his card in the box before taking a seat in the front row, his shoulders straight but not rigid.

Eli watched him go, then looked at the blank card in front of him. His hand trembled as he picked up the pen, a simple blue Bic that somehow felt weighted with possibility. The words came slowly, his handwriting shakier than usual.

God, I don't know what I'm doing anymore. I used to think I had a plan, but nothing worked out. Please show me where I belong. Help me believe You still see me. He stared at the words, feeling exposed and relieved at the same time. Then folded the card twice. He folded the card again, creating a small, private package of hope.

The walk to the front felt longer than it should have. Each step on the hardwood spoke softly, but no one looked up. When he slipped the card into the box, the wood was warm under his fingers, worn smooth by countless other desperate prayers. He exhaled, and something shifted inside his chest. It wasn't resolution. It wasn't a lightning bolt of clarity. It was permission. It was permission to not have everything figured out. The first step simply was to ask.

To believe that maybe, just maybe, showing up was enough for now.

As he turned to leave, his eyes caught a bulletin board near the exit, a mosaic of community announcements, prayer requests, and opportunities. A bright yellow flyer read:

Outreach Day: Saturday, 9 a.m. Helpers Needed. Contact: Leah Thompson. He tore off the bottom tab with her number and placed it in his pocket, the paper crinkling softly. Just in case, hope was something you could practice. Two days later, Eli found himself back at Grace Commons. This time outside in the mild morning air, wearing work gloves Leah had loaned him and standing beside Jacob, a barista-turned-blogger he vaguely recognized from The Daily Grind coffee shop downtown.

They were both assigned to setup duty, unfolding tables and arranging chairs for the community meal that would follow the morning's service activities. "You're the guy from prayer night, right?" Jacob asked, his voice carrying the easy familiarity of someone who'd also been changed by that evening. "Back row, gray sweatshirt?" Eli nodded, taken aback by the memory. "Yeah, that's me." Jacob smiled as he adjusted a table leg. "Me too. That box gave me a sense of permission to stop pretending I had everything figured out.

"Yeah," Eli said, lifting his end of the table. "Me too." They worked in comfortable silence for a while, the rhythm of setup giving their hands something to do while their minds processed. It wasn't awkward; it was steady and on purpose. It was the type of work that evoked a sense of moving prayer. At the end of the day, as people shared pizza and laughter around folding tables, Eli found himself sitting beside Elias again. The older man was listening to a young mother tell a story about her toddler, his attention full and genuine.

When she moved on to refill her plate, Elias turned to Eli with a knowing smile. "Back for more?" he asked. "I think..." Eli paused, watching Jacob serve pizza to a group of teenagers with effortless grace, seeing Leah coordinate cleanup with the kind of joy that came from knowing your purpose. "I think I'm starting to believe this matters. That maybe I matter." Elias nodded slowly, his eyes crinkling with satisfaction. "It always mattered, son. You just needed to see it. Occasionally we have to step into the story before we can read our part."

And perhaps Eli was beginning to understand that belonging wasn't something you earned. It was something that must be accepted. Something you practiced. It began as a whispered prayer and grew into a purposeful action.

The radio in his heart was finally finding its frequency.

"What lies behind us and what lies before us are tiny matters compared to what lies within us."

Ralph Waldo Emerson

Eli was getting a better sense of what his purpose was, like how fog slowly lifts from a valley at dawn. It used to be something far away and difficult to catch, like a cloud or a question he couldn't quite answer. But now, for the first time in a long time, the edges were starting to get sharper and take shape. A sudden realization didn't hit him like a bolt of lightning. Instead, it was more like the first rays of sunlight peeking through a curtain at dawn, warming his skin just enough to tell him that there was still light in the world.

Eli stopped waiting for the big sign at some point and didn't even know it. He would rather not see fireworks or hear a loud voice in the sky. In its place, he started to notice the small, daily things that seemed to hold hidden meaning. There was no mountain behind him or a faraway future where his purpose was hidden. His purpose was found in the present moment, specifically in the breath he was taking.

Things that didn't seem important before, like being there for a friend, listening, or even just going about his daily life, now had meaning. They weren't just fun things to do; they were important things to do. Every small choice to be there, to be kind, to just "be" was like a puzzle piece fitting together slowly but surely. He learned that the purpose wasn't about finding the "right" road but about walking the one in front of you.

In the past, Eli thought that his purpose came from above and that he had to be good enough to deserve it. But now he was beginning to view it as something that could be cultivated. It was something that could be grown with every thought, action, and choice.

It was in the way he saw the world and the people in it, as well as the way he decided to live each day. It was no longer necessary for him to wait for permission to live his purpose. Piece by piece, he was living it.

He was also beginning to understand why he didn't have it all together. He used to feel guilty and ashamed because he thought he wasn't doing or being enough. He didn't have to know everything for it to matter. He wasn't feeling rushed to have his life planned out. It was fine to not have all the puzzle pieces together yet; the doubt wasn't a failure; it was just a part of the trip. And in that doubt, his purpose was changing in ways he hadn't planned.

Being there was just as important as doing. In the little things, Eli learned that there was meaning. The more caring way he listened, the more he helped without expecting anything in return, and the more he let himself feel things, even when they were difficult. It was less about the "end goal" and more about the "process," the path of finding meaning in the here and now, in small moments that didn't seem important at first.

Eli felt like he was living on purpose for the first time, just the way he was. He didn't wait for something or someone to change; instead, he found meaning in the life he was already living. And the more he believed that, the more his way became clear. Not because he knew everything, but because he no longer needed to.

Reflective Questions

1. Have you ever felt like an outsider in a spiritual setting? What was your emotional response, and what one small step could you take to move towards belonging in a similar situation now?

2. What is one silent prayer you've held in your heart but never spoken? Consider how you might begin to voice or act on that unspoken desire.

3. How do you typically handle the tension between doubt and faith? What is one small action you could take to practice faith despite your doubt this week?

4. Identify someone in your life who offers gentle nudges toward growth or healing. How can you acknowledge or reciprocate that support?

Scripture for Reflection

Jeremiah 29:13
'You will seek me and find me when you seek me with all your heart.'

Psalm 34:18
'The Lord is close to the brokenhearted and saves those who are crushed in spirit.'

Hebrews 11:6
'And without faith it is impossible to please God... he rewards those who earnestly seek him.

Matthew 6:6
'But when you pray, go into your room, close the door, and pray to your Father, who is unseen.'

2

COFFEE, COURAGE & THE CALL

Fueling Faith Facing Fear

Ecclesiastes 11:4 (NIV)
"Whoever watches the wind will not plant; whoever looks at the clouds will not reap."

Jacob Hartman believed in two things: excellent coffee and quiet corners. That's why, even on busy weekends, you'd find him hidden in the back of Willow & Elm Café, scribbling in his leather-bound notebook, earbuds in, but not playing music. He needed the silence to think, to process, and to remember why words mattered. He worked the morning shift five days a week, up at 4:30 a.m. to prep the espresso machine, grinding beans that filled the air with rich, earthy promises. The familiar ritual of steaming milk and pulling shots had become a kind of meditation. Officially, he was a barista. Unofficially, he was a storyteller in hiding.

Jacob had grown up in Grace Commons. He was baptized at twelve years old in the old sanctuary before it was renovated. By the age of fifteen, he worked as a sound technician, learning to balance microphones and mix hymns with contemporary praise songs. He became a poet by eighteen, although no one was aware of that aspect of his life. His journals were filled with devotionals that asked challenging questions, half-finished blog posts about faith and doubt, and story drafts that captured the sacred in everyday moments. But they had never seen the light of day. He was terrified of being misunderstood. Alternatively, the fear could stem from people's indifference and lack of concern.

The fear had roots. In high school, he'd submitted a piece about his grandfather's death to the school literary magazine. His English teacher had read it aloud to the class as an example of "overwrought sentimentality." The laughter that followed had lingered in his chest for years, making him protective of anything that mattered too much. So when his friend Leah casually said, "You should share what you write," his instinctive answer was always, "Maybe later." Later felt safer than now.

It was a Wednesday when Leah stopped by his café with a flyer, her cheeks flushed from the October wind. The afternoon rush had died down, leaving only the soft creak of the espresso machine and the gentle clatter of a few customers typing on laptops.

"Outreach Day:

We need volunteers," she said, sliding the bright yellow paper across the counter, her eyes twinkling with the kind of mischief that usually meant trouble for Jacob's comfort zone. Jacob glanced at the flyer, then back at his espresso machine, using the steam wand to create perfect microfoam, a skill that had taken him two years to master. "I don't know, Leah. Saturdays are my writing days." "Exactly," she said, leaning against the counter with the confidence of someone who'd known him since youth group. "This might be the kind of interruption your writing needs. When was the last time you wrote about something that actually happened instead of something you imagined?"

He raised an eyebrow, wiping down the counter with more force than necessary. "That sounds like spiritual manipulation." She grinned, stealing a piece of biscotti from the display case. "It is. But it's also true. You've been writing about faith and community for years. Maybe it's time to experience it." Jacob felt the familiar tightness in his chest, the same feeling he got when he hovered over the "publish" button on his blog drafts. "What if I'm terrible at it?" "Then you'll have something honest to write about," Leah said, taking a bite of biscotti. "Besides, you're not terrible at anything. You're just terrified of being human in front of people."

On Saturday, Jacob arrived early, notebook still in his backpack, like a security blanket. The morning air was clean and carried the scent of fallen leaves and possibility. He was assigned to the welcome table with a guy named Eli, a quiet man who seemed more introverted than he was, which was saying something. They clicked quickly, both comfortable with long silences and the kind of work that didn't require small talk. "You're the guy who writes?" Eli asked mid-morning, while they restocked pamphlets about the church's community programs.

Jacob's eyes widened, his hands stilling on the stack of papers. "How'd you know?" "I saw your name on a blog once. Something about struggling with prayer. Didn't know it was yours until Leah told me this morning." Jacob tensed, the familiar heat of exposure spreading up his neck. "You read it?" "Yeah," Eli said, his voice gentle and matter-of-fact. "The one about feeling like your prayers bounce off the ceiling. I liked it. Made me feel less alone." Jacob nodded slowly, surprised by the relief that washed over him. "Thanks. I haven't posted anything in months."

"Why not?" He shrugged, organizing the pamphlets with unnecessary precision. "Analysis paralysis, mostly. I write something, then convince myself it's not good enough, not helpful enough, not... enough." Eli smiled knowingly, the kind of smile that came from personal experience. "I overthink brushing my teeth. But I'm learning that faith isn't about getting it perfect. It's about showing up. Even when you're shaking." Later that day, while handing out water bottles to families loading groceries into their cars, Jacob found himself watching the intricate dance of community. The volunteers moved with purpose, some naturally gifted at organization, others at conversation, and still others at the quiet work of loading boxes. The families receiving food boxes carried their dignity, their stories, and their quiet strength.

It was messy and beautiful. Raw and holy. He watched a little girl help her grandmother carry a bag of apples, their hands intertwined. He saw teenagers from the youth group high-fiving kids half their age. He noticed how Eli, despite his earlier claims of social anxiety, was making easy conversation with an elderly man about woodworking. His fingers began to itch, like the familiar sensation that came when words were building up inside him, demanding to be written.

That night, back at the café after closing, Jacob sat in his usual corner booth. The room seemed more personal and honest in the dark. The faint aroma of the lavender cleaning solution he used on the tables blended with the lingering smell of coffee grounds and vanilla syrup.

He opened his notebook, his pen hovering over the blank page. The post practically wrote itself.

"The Courage to Begin (Or: How I Learned to Stop Hiding Behind Perfect)"

I've spent most of my adult life waiting for the right moment to share my voice. The moment when I'd have something profound to say, when my words would be polished enough, when I'd be brave enough to handle whatever response came. Today I realized that moment doesn't exist. I spent Saturday morning at a community outreach event, watching real faith in action. Not the kind that posts inspirational quotes on social media, but the kind that shows up early to fold tables and stays late to sweep crumbs. I watched people who didn't have it all figured out serving people who were in the middle of figuring it out.

> *"Courage is the most important of all the virtues, because without courage, you can't practice any other virtue consistently."*
>
> **Maya Angelou**

And I understood something: courage isn't the absence of fear. It's moving forward with shaking hands. We keep waiting for someone else, God or some other version of ourselves who is flawless, to grant us permission to start. But what if the permission is in the beginning itself? What if showing up imperfectly is better than hiding perfectly? Today I'm choosing to begin. Not because I'm ready, but because readiness is overrated.

Because someone needs to hear that it's okay to be nervous, to doubt, and to try anyway.

This is me, trying anyway. Jacob stared at the words, his heart hammering against his ribs. He read them again and again, making minor edits and second-guessing every sentence. His cursor floated over the "publish" button for ten minutes. His palms were sweating. He thought about Eli's words, about Leah's challenge, and about the little girl helping her grandmother with apples. He closed his eyes and clicked. The next morning, Jacob almost threw up. He'd barely slept, checking his phone every few minutes, then forcing himself to put it down, then checking again. By 6 AM, he gave up on sleep and went to work early, losing himself in the familiar rhythm of grinding beans and heating milk.

But by noon, his blog had been shared a dozen times. By Sunday, the number had reached fifty. The responses trickled in throughout the day. Some were simple hearts and thumbs-up emojis. Others were longer and more personal. A young woman messaged him: "I've been sitting on my dream of opening an art studio for three years. I finally called regarding that lease space downtown because of your post. An older man commented, "I retired two years ago and have been afraid to volunteer anywhere because I don't know what I'm doing. After reading your post, I decided to sign up for three volunteer opportunities. Thank you."

> *"Do it scared. It's okay to feel the fear, but do it anyway."*
> **Ruth Soukup**

A mother wrote, "My daughter keeps asking to quit piano because she's not good enough yet. I'm showing her this post. Occasionally, our kids need to see us try imperfectly, too." Jacob stared at the messages, tears stinging his eyes. He'd spent so long afraid of his words not mattering that he'd never considered they might matter too much, that they might actually change something for someone. He didn't need a massive platform. He just needed to start. At church that Sunday, Pastor Evelyn stopped him in the hallway after service, her eyes bright with the kind of excitement that made Jacob simultaneously honored and terrified.

"That post of yours," she said, gripping his arm gently, "was a sermon in pixels. You captured something I've been trying to preach for months." Jacob laughed nervously, running his hand through his hair. "It was terrifying to post." "That's how you know it's worth doing," she said. "The things that scare us are usually the things God wants to use.

"Fear is just excitement without breath."

Two weeks later, Pastor Evelyn asked him to speak at the next First Friday gathering, a monthly event where community members shared stories, talents, and testimonies.

"Just five minutes," she said, as if that made it less terrifying. "Tell them what you told us in that post. About beginning before you're ready." Jacob's immediate instinct was to decline. Speaking in front of people felt like taking his already vulnerable writing and amplifying it through a microphone.

But the responses to his blog post had been replaying in his mind, about how people were stepping out of their comfort zones because of something he'd written. He thought about the woman calling about the art studio lease. The man is signing up to volunteer. The mother showed her daughter that trying imperfectly was better than not trying at all.

His mouth opened to say no. Instead, he heard himself say, "Yes."

First Friday came too quickly. Jacob stood behind the small stage in the fellowship hall, his hands shaking as he held index cards with bullet points he'd written and rewritten a dozen times. The room was full but not packed, maybe sixty people scattered across folding chairs, nursing coffee and conversation. His heart pounded so hard he was sure the microphone would pick it up. When Pastor Evelyn introduced him, he walked to the front on legs that felt disconnected from his body. The microphone seemed impossibly tall, the lights impossibly bright.

He looked out at the faces in the hall, some familiar, some new, yet all expectant. He conveyed the truth. He talked about hiding behind perfection. He talked about waiting for permission that never materialized. He discussed the fear that had prevented him from speaking and the community that had given him the courage to do so. "I'm not up here because I have it all figured out," he said, his voice steadier than he felt. "I'm up here because I'm still figuring it out, and maybe that's exactly what some of you need to hear." When he finished, the applause was warm and genuine. But more than that, people persisted afterward. They told him their own stories of creative dreams deferred, of calls they'd been afraid to answer, and of words they'd been afraid to speak.

An elderly woman, Mrs. Chen, approached him with tears in her eyes. "I've been writing letters to my grandchildren in Taiwan for thirty years," she said. "I always thought they were too simple, too ordinary. But you've made me think... Maybe ordinary is enough." Afterward, someone asked him, "When's your next post?" Jacob smiled, the fear still there but no longer paralyzing. "Soon," he said. "I have a lot to say."

Jacob stood in awe, wondering about the repercussions if he had not said yes to the opportunity to speak about courage in the presence of fear. He wondered at all the testimonies and how his writings had motivated many to pursue their dreams and challenge their fears.

Jacob concluded that failing to manifest our gifts is more damaging, as many people depend on our courage and actions.

His words helped others discover their way through dark places where hope seemed weak. They guided those lost in the shadows, demonstrating a path forward even during the most challenging times. His message wasn't just one of support; it was also a call to action: to face fears, navigate the unknown, and keep going even when things get tough.

Do what Jacob did. When your feet feel like they can't handle it, take a brave step forward. Trust your gut and do it anyway, because that's when you grow the most. You should keep going even if you don't know everything. Have faith that the process will teach you what you need to know. Every mistake, failure, and moment of doubt prepares you for what's next. And act like it could be your last chance, because when you treat life like that, you start to value every step, every moment, and every opportunity.

Don't wait until everything is just right. Don't hold back until you understand. Leave right away. Move around. Not only will you find your way, but you'll also gain the strength to show others the way.

Reflective Questions

1. Could you share something you've hesitated to begin due to concerns about achieving perfection? What is one imperfect step you could take to begin this week?

2. How does fear of judgment impact your ability to share your gifts or message? What is one small truth you could share this week, even if it feels vulnerable?

3. Identify someone you could encourage this week to begin something they've been putting off. How will you reach out and offer specific encouragement?

4. Envision stepping out in faith this week, even if you're unsure of the outcome. What would be the smallest possible courageous act you could perform?

Scripture for Reflection

Ecclesiastes 11:4
'Whoever watches the wind will not plant; whoever looks at the clouds will not reap

2 Timothy 1:7
'For the Spirit God gave us does not make us timid, but gives us power, love, and self-discipline.

James 2:17
'In the same way, faith by itself, if it is not accompanied by action, is dead.

Proverbs 16:3
'Commit to the Lord whatever you do, and he will establish your plans.'

3

HEART IN MOTION

Trusting God With Every step

Proverbs 16:3 (NIV)
"Commit to the Lord whatever you do, and he will establish your plans."

Leah Simmons-Thompson was the oldest of four girls, born into a family where faith was stitched into every corner of their small Alabama home. Her father pastored a modest church set between farmland and gravel roads, the kind of congregation where the potluck calendar was sacred and news traveled faster than the choir could sing it. Her mother, equal parts prayer warrior and choir director, raised her daughters on Proverbs, hymns, and a steady belief that leadership was simply service dressed in purpose.

Leadership came naturally to Leah. As a child, she directed her sisters in backyard plays; in youth group, she was the organizer; in college ministries, she became the one people looked to for direction without her ever asking for it. Her energy inspired people, her decisiveness steadied them, and her ability to see three steps ahead made her an indispensable leader. She coordinated food drives, mission trips, and volunteer teams with equal parts structure and heart.

But leadership wasn't effortless. Not really. Because underneath her poise lived a deep, pulsing fear.

A fear of failing.

A fear of disappointing others.

A fear that things might fall apart and that she would be to blame.

That fear had roots.

When she was fifteen, her father's church split after misplaced trust in one of the leaders. Leah remembered the night clearly: the hallway dim, her parents' voices low, heavy with grief. She stood silently, listening.

Leah never forgot hearing her father whisper, "Maybe I should have seen it coming," and her mother softly replied, "We did our best." Those words sank into her like stones, sowing a belief that failure wasn't just painful but devastating. It hurt the people you loved. It left scars on communities.

The following Sunday, half the pews sat empty. Her father tried to preach about forgiveness, but his voice trembled. Leah sat beside her sisters with a hardness growing in her chest. She made a private vow that day: never let anything fall apart again. If she could hold things together, she would. If she could prevent heartbreak, she must. Control became her way of protecting everyone, especially herself.

Those early moments shaped her understanding of leadership. To Leah, excellence was a shield.

Then Caleb Thompson entered her world.

He was the opposite of her. The mood changed because he was calm, slow, and kind. Leah ran as fast as she could, but Caleb walked slowly on purpose. He asked her questions she had never thought of before, like, "What if rest is also obedience?" And, "What if God moves just as strongly when things aren't perfect?"

They met during a college volunteer project. Assigned to pack hygiene kits, Leah sped through her task while Caleb worked at a peaceful rhythm, humming quietly to himself.

Caleb had smiled at her and said, "You pack like you're trying to save the world in one afternoon." She rolled her eyes, but what he said stuck with her long after she got home. The peace he carried with him made her feel as if she were being invited to something she didn't know how to accept.

Their early relationship had its friction.

Once, after a service project that didn't meet her expectations, Leah vented to Caleb about every detail that had gone wrong. He listened quietly before responding, "You know you don't have to fix everything, right?"

No one had ever said that to her. The words felt uncomfortable, like trying to wear a new shoe that didn't fit yet but promised to someday.

Together they made a strong team, but as their ministry expanded, so did Leah's desire to keep every moving part perfect. She wanted excellence. She also wanted to outrun the ghost of that church split that had happened all those years ago.

Outreach Day:

The most significant event she had ever coordinated became the proving ground.

The entire week before Outreach Day felt like running a race without a finish line. Leah stayed up late making lists, organizing volunteers, and sending reminder texts and emails with subject lines like "Just double-checking!" and "Confirming one last thing!"She could tell her team was tired, but she kept going anyway.

She had even overheard Jacob tell Zara, "She means well... but she doesn't let anyone breathe." The words stung, but Leah shrugged them off. She told herself it was her job to keep things together. Letting go felt too much like inviting failure.

The night before the event, Leah lay awake replaying every worst-case scenario. What if the vendors were late? What if the crowd was small? What if people judged their ministry harshly?

It wasn't just logistics she was trying to control. It was the fear of reliving the heartbreak she saw in her parents' eyes years ago.

The next morning, Caleb made blueberry pancakes, which are her favorite.

Leah sat at the table, laptop open, scrolling through messages, untouched food in front of her.

Caleb gently closed her laptop.

"It's going to be beautiful," he said.

She shook her head.

"That's what I'm afraid of. What if beauty isn't enough? What if perfect isn't enough?"

By mid-morning, everything unraveled.

The food truck ended up at the wrong church across town.

Two volunteers argued about table placement.

Children ran everywhere.

The bounce house deflated in front of a crowd of disappointed kids.

A vendor insisted he never received payment receipts.

The sun pressed down harder than Leah expected. She could feel sweat soak through her shirt as she tried to manage four problems at once. Her chest tightened. Her heart raced. Her inner voice screamed, "Keep it together. If the effort fails, it's on you."

She snapped at Caleb.

She snapped at volunteers.

Zara, the new single mother who was volunteering for the first time, was the target of Leah's tense words.

"Where do you want these markers?" Zara asked gently.

"Just put them somewhere! Anywhere! Please use common sense! " Leah barked back.

Zara's face fell immediately. She stepped back as if she had been struck. Guilt crashed through Leah, but she was too busy trying to fix everything to apologize. She felt the day slipping through her fingers like water she couldn't hold.

Caleb came over with a bottle of water.

"What if you didn't have to handle it all?" he asked.

She brushed him aside.

"I'll handle it. I always do."

Inside, she felt as if she were drowning.

"No speaker? How am I going to explain this?" Leah muttered.

Jacob stepped forward. "I could share something… from my blog," he said timidly.

Caleb touched her arm.

"What if this is God's plan?"

Jacob walked onto the small stage, trembling.

"I'm nervous," he began, "but sometimes God shows up in the places we least expect, even in the mistakes we try to hide."

His voice got stronger. A lot of people leaned in. Tears came out.

For the first time that day, Leah stopped moving. She stopped fixing. She let herself breathe and watch.

 Caleb wrapped an arm around her waist.

Applause rose like a wave. Leah saw the event with new eyes.

Later, under string lights, she found Zara wiping tables.

"I owe you an apology," Leah said.

Zara sniffed. "I felt useful today."

"You weren't useful," Leah said. "You were a blessing."

"Would you join our planning team?"

"I'd love that."

Fear wasn't a sign to stop.

Fear usually meant something meaningful was about to happen.

"Let's make it happen," Leah told Caleb.

"I'm with you," he said.

This time, Leah experienced a renewed sense of vitality. Not perfect, but real.

And sometimes, real is enough to change the world one brave step at a time.

Reflection Questions

1. Where are you clinging to control out of fear?

2. Who is waiting for an invitation into purpose?

3. What would it look like to let God surprise you?

4. How can you practice gratitude instead of perfection?

Scriptures For Reflection

Proverbs 16:3
"Commit to the Lord whatever you do, and he will establish your plans."

2 Timothy 1:7
"For the Spirit God gave us does not make us timid, but gives us power, love, and self-discipline."

Ecclesiastes 11:4
"Whoever watches the wind will not plant; whoever looks at the clouds will not reap."

James 2:17
"In the same way, faith by itself, if it is not accompanied by action, is dead."

4

BEAUTIFULLY BROKEN, GRACEFULLY WHOLE

Healing in the Hands of Grace

Romans 8:1 (NIV)
"There is therefore now no condemnation for those who are in Christ Jesus."

Podcasting was never Zara Martinez's original career goal. Those dreams belonged to people with time, people who woke up to calm mornings and neatly organized calendars. Those dreams did not belong to single mothers who spent their days rushing from daycare drop-offs to late-night shifts, juggling two jobs, three schedules, and a thousand invisible responsibilities that no one ever saw but everyone depended on.

On most days, her only goal was to survive until bedtime with enough strength left to whisper a tired prayer.

When her son Micah laughed, it filled her with life. But when he fell asleep, the silence often felt too heavy, so heavy that it pressed on the parts of her she tried to ignore. In those quiet moments after midnight, she found herself scribbling in a battered notebook. Not poetry. Not dreams. She was filled with raw prayers and confessions, too exhausted to speak aloud.

There was no filter. No polish. Just the truth.

The truth was painful and unedited.

Occasionally, the words poured out so fast her hand shook. Other times, she wrote so slowly it felt like bleeding. "Lord, I'm tired." "Lord, I'm scared." "Lord, why does he get to walk away, and I'm the one picking up the pieces? "

Those pages were meant to be a private and sacred conversation between her and God, who sometimes felt silent but never absent.

But over the months, something changed.

She felt something move. A soft voice. She tried to ignore the gentle push.

Can you imagine that your story may inspire someone else?

Her pulse raced. She had no platform. No confidence. No time. And her voice? Trembling.
Barely there.

What if no one cared?
What if her brokenness was too exposed?
What if people judged her?

But the stirring would not stop. It followed her into the shower, her car, and her prayers. It was so persistent, so constant, like a heartbeat begging to be heard.

Finally, one night, she gave in.

She recorded her first podcast episode in her tiny, dimly lit kitchen, using a borrowed microphone and her phone stacked on top of two cereal boxes. Micah slept in the next room. The hum of the refrigerator became her soundtrack.

Her voice shook as she told the truth.

About Devon leaving.
About the shame she wore like a second skin.
About nights when loneliness suffocated her.
About feeling like a failure as a woman, a mother, and a believer.

She nearly deleted it afterward.

She kept hovering over the delete button, heart racing, sweating through her t-shirt as she whispered, "God… I don't want to be seen like this."

But trembling, she hit publish.

By the end of the week, over 700 people had shared the episode. Messages poured in from places she had never been, from voices she never expected.

A woman from Texas wrote, "I was going to give up on dating. I thought I was too damaged to love. Your honesty reminded me I'm still healing."

A single father from Michigan said, "I've been hiding from my kids emotionally since my divorce. Your story helped me realize they need to see me healing, not pretending."

A pastor's wife wrote,
"Thank you. I've never admitted out loud that I feel broken, too."

As Zara read each message, something awakened inside her, something she hadn't felt since before Devon walked out.

A purpose that didn't feel forced or borrowed or manufactured. A purpose born from her wounds, breathing through her story, calling her to rise.

Tears streamed down her face. She lifted her hands in worship right there in her kitchen, surrounded by dirty dishes and unfolded laundry.

She had survived the kind of heartbreak people didn't talk about. She had endured nights when the weight of raising Micah alone felt unbearable.
She had kept going even when she felt unworthy, unwanted, and unseen.

Grace held her up. Imperfect, scarred, but standing.

And she realized that her survival wasn't accidental. It was intentional. It was divine. God had been holding her together in places she thought had fallen apart.

She thought about all the women who hid their pain because they were afraid of judgment. The mothers who suffered silently. The dreamers who believed their mistakes disqualified them. She knew their shame too well.

Time had always been her enemy.

Between work, parenting, and surviving daily life, how could she pour into others?

But God can multiply even the smallest offering. She started recording five-minute clips between loads of laundry, during Micah's naps, and at red lights. In the moments most people rushed through, God was building a ministry she never asked for but desperately needed.

Then came the message that reconnected her.

A young woman wrote, "I had planned to take my life tonight. Something, or God, I guess, told me to listen to your episode first. Thank you for saving me."

Zara dropped to her knees, heaving sobs.

This was not a podcast anymore. It was a task, a goal, and a response from God to someone's desperate prayer.

People from all over began to share their hearts:
Young adults who felt lost began to share their stories.
Men who had never expressed their pain began to share their hearts.
Mothers drowning in shame began to share their stories.
Older people are grieving lifelong regrets.

Each testimony reminded her: God uses the broken.

Her joy wasn't loud. It was deep, like water settling in the soul.

She realized her broken pieces weren't proof of failure. They were proof of God's gentle, redeeming hand at work.

Zara lingered to tidy up after a Thursday night small-group meeting at Grace Commons. Quiet, considerate, and soft-spoken, Eli offered to assist with chair stacking.

They had met at Outreach Day but had never exchanged more than a passing smile.

"I heard your podcast," he said, voice steady. "Thank you for sharing that."

Heat rushed to her cheeks.
"I almost backed out three times," she admitted.

Eli let out a breath, as if he had been holding his story inside. "I know what that's like," he said, "to feel like your voice is too shaky to matter."

She gave him a serious look and noticed the bruised hope in his eyes.

"Do you… think it's too late for someone like me?" she asked softly. "To start over? To believe in good things again?"

Eli's reply was gentle but solid.
"I think people like you help the rest of us find our way back. You're proof that healing is possible."

It was the first time in years she felt seen, not as broken, but as becoming.

That night, after Micah fell asleep, Zara sat in her living room listening to the rain tap against the window. Their small apartment, which used to remind her of everything she had lost, now felt like a safe place.

She opened her journal and wrote:

"God, thank you for teaching me that broken doesn't mean useless. Thank you for loving me through the shame I thought would swallow me. Thank you for turning the pieces I hate into a testimony of your faithfulness."

"I am whole," she wrote, "not because the pain is gone, but because you are with me in it."

She whispered Psalm 34:18 out loud, her voice steady:

"The Lord is close to the brokenhearted."

She came to realize that God had not only been present during her most difficult times, but had also been working quietly and tenderly in them.

Micah stirred in his sleep, and a soft smile spread across her face.

Her son had been her anchor, her joy, and her glimpse of God's unwavering strength. Every day, her faith grew, not because her life was perfect, but because God was perfect in her imperfection.

What began as a story of heartbreak had become a story of redemption.

A ministry was born not from strength, but from surrender. Not from perfection, but from brokenness.

God doesn't require perfection.
Just willing.

And Zara?
She had finally become willing.

Reflection Questions

1. What broken piece of your story do you still believe makes you unusable? How might God be inviting you to see it as part of your healing?
2. Where could your vulnerability become someone else's bridge back to hope?
3. Who in your life needs to hear the unfiltered truth of your journey, not a polished speech, but the truth of your journey?
4. What would it look like to trust that wholeness isn't the absence of scars, but God's presence in the midst of them?

Scriptures for Reflection

Romans 8:1
"There is therefore now no condemnation for those who are in Christ Jesus."

Isaiah 61:3
"...to give them beauty for ashes, the oil of joy for mourning..."

Joel 2:25
"I will restore to you the years that the swarming locust has eaten."

Psalm 34:18
"The Lord is close to the brokenhearted and saves those who are crushed in spirit."

5

FAITH ON FIRE

From Spark to Flame

2 Timothy 1:6 (NIV)
"Fan into flame the gift of God, which is in you."

James Wallace had always understood the language of construction: the beat of a hammer on wood, the buzz of saws shaping raw material, and the satisfying click of pieces fitting perfectly together. His hands moved with the confidence of someone who had spent years mastering the silent art of creation. Wood, metal, drywall, and electrical wire. They were stories waiting for a builder's touch.

He could fix almost anything. He could fix things that were broken, like a light switch that didn't work, a table leg that was split, or a wobbly cabinet. James could fix anything that was broken. He didn't just repair; he restored.

Even as a child, James had been drawn to broken things. When other kids played with toys, he took them apart to see how they worked. He remembered sitting on the floor beside his grandfather, watching him sand a piece of oak until it shone like new. "Everything can be fixed," his grandfather had said. "Some things just need more patience than others." Those words became James's first gospel of hope that brokenness wasn't an ending. It was an invitation.

His days were spent quietly serving others, installing ceiling fans for Mrs. Chen next door, repairing loose railings for seniors, and replacing lighting for new families in the community. Mrs. Chen always baked him lemon bars, and while he worked, she chatted about her garden, her grandkids, and her memories of immigrating to the States. To her, James wasn't just a handyman. He was a steady presence. He served as a constant reminder that kindness could still be both simple and practical.

But when it was time for James to build something that really mattered to him, he froze.

His brain worked differently. He could see solutions in three dimensions, understand how systems connected instinctively, and turn disorder into structure. But the world cared about degrees and credentials. He lasted one semester in community college.

He remembered the humiliation of sitting in a math class where the professor spoke too fast, the room was too loud, and his mind was too crowded. He remembered leaving the building mid-lecture, sweaty and lightheaded, knowing he could not force himself into a system that didn't speak his language. His counselor's disappointed headshake stung more than the failure.

It wasn't just a class he dropped out of; it felt like he had fallen out of the future everyone else expected of him. Still, beneath the doubt, a quiet dream flickered—a space for young men like him.
Skilled with their hands.
Overlooked by the world.

He even had a name for it: Build Brothers. A place where men could learn trades, discover their worth, and build confidence one project at a time. But he never spoke about it, not after what happened three years ago. At a community development meeting, he had suggested offering introductory trade workshops to teens. They brushed him aside.

He remembered the exact moment: the chairperson looked at his rough hands, then at his plain work boots, and said, "Let's stick to realistic ideas." Everyone chuckled. James sat frozen, feeling the heat of shame crawl up his face. He left before the meeting ended and promised never to speak up again.

So he fixed things, stayed quiet, and kept his dream buried under layers of doubt. One evening, while working under a sink at the church, Jacob appeared with two cups of coffee.

"Watching you work is like watching an artist," Jacob said.

James chuckled. "It's just a sink."

Jacob shook his head. "No. It's a calling.

Why haven't you launched that mentoring program you told me about?"

James hesitated. "Nobody takes a dropout seriously."

Jacob leaned back against the counter.
"You don't need an MBA," he said. "You need a message. And you have one: dignity through craft, purpose through building, and community through teaching. That's revolutionary."

James swallowed hard.

The word "revolutionary" felt too big for him. Too heavy. Too holy. He had spent years shrinking back, and now someone was asking him to grow. Growing was painful for him because he wasn't accustomed to being seen.

A week later, Leah handed him a flyer for a community pitch night. James shoved it back quickly.

"Nope. I'm not getting laughed out of a building again."Pastor Evelyn, overhearing, walked over."James," she said, her voice steady and warm, "if God gave you the vision, He'll fund it with favor. But favor requires showing up. Every time you help Micah. Every time you volunteer. Every time you fix something for a neighbor. You're already mentoring. You just haven't named it yet."

Her words landed like scripture.

They sank into places he didn't talk about, the parts of him still wounded by dismissal, still haunted by feeling 'not enough.' It felt like God was speaking directly through her, calling out what he buried.

The night of the pitch, James almost didn't come.

Zara intercepted him at the door, grabbed his folder, and said, "You're overthinking. Wear the flannel. It's you."

He laughed despite himself.

The fellowship hall glowed under string lights. The smell of Pastor Evelyn's famous cookies filled the air. Young entrepreneurs pitched sleek apps, boutique gyms, and modern cafés. James sat in the back row, palms sweating, rehearsing his introduction under his breath.

When his name was called, his legs felt like wood.

As he walked to the front, he heard his heart pound louder than the applause. He couldn't stop his hands from shaking. He couldn't stop the memory of being laughed at three years ago. For a split second, he thought about turning around and leaving.

But then he saw Micah peeking from behind Zara's leg, giving a big thumbs-up.

James inhaled deeply.

"My name is James Wallace," he began, voice trembling. "I fix things."

People chuckled softly.

He continued.

"I fix furniture that is broken." Lights that don't work. Railings that are broken. But lately, I've seen something else that's broken: people. Young men who feel like they're not enough. Older people who can't afford repairs. A community that's lost the skills we used to pass down with pride."

He held up his hands.
"These hands? They've built for fifteen years. I don't have charts or projections. But I have a belief that every person carries value if given the chance to learn."

There was no sound. Then, a roaring round of applause.

Offers poured in: funding, mentorship, referrals, and partnerships.

Pastor Evelyn's eyes shimmered with pride.

For the first time, James didn't feel like just a handyman.

He felt like a builder of futures.

A Dream Built in Real Time

Three weeks later, sunlight streamed into the garage that would become Build Brothers' first workshop.

Eli measured wood for benches.
Jacob scribbled notes for a blog titled "Building Men, One Board at a Time."
Zara sorted tools while Micah "helped" with oversized screws.
Neighbors dropped off supplies and snacks.

Hope hung in the air like sawdust.

Leah came up beside James.
"This all started because you believed your gifts mattered. There is nothing that God throws away; not students who drop out of school, not pipes that break, and not dreams that seem to be too big for the person who has them.

James ran a hand across a donated workbench.

He was able to recall every instance of uncertainty, including every person who disregarded him, every job interview in which he felt insignificant, and every instance in which he concealed his ideas out of fear. And now here he stood, surrounded by people who believed in him before he believed in himself.

"I thought I needed permission to matter," he said quietly. "Turns out I just needed to remember I already did."

The foundation was laid.

Now the real building could begin.

Reflection Questions

1. What dream have you shelved because you didn't think you were qualified?
2. Where have others' definitions of success silenced your gifts?
3. Who could you empower by sharing your vision and inviting them into it?
4. How might you fan your faith into fire through obedience rather than perfection?

Scriptures for Reflection

2 Timothy 1:6
"Fan into flame the gift of God, which is in you."

Exodus 4:10–12
"I will help you speak and will teach you what to say."

1 Corinthians 1:27
"God chose the foolish things of the world to shame the wise."

Proverbs 16:3
"Commit to the Lord whatever you do, and he will establish your plans."

6

WAITING WELL

Courage in the Pause

Psalm 27:14 (NIV)
"Wait on the Lord; be of good courage, and He shall strengthen your heart; wait, I say, on the Lord!"

Pastor Evelyn Ross had blessed more weddings than she could count. She had steadied shaky hands at altars, prayed over trembling voices, and offered tiny truths about choosing one another on ordinary Tuesdays. She had watched couples stand in freshly ironed suits and expensive lace, declaring forever with optimism that sometimes made her smile and sometimes made her ache.

But when the sanctuary emptied and the lights clicked off, she often slipped quietly into the third pew on the right, the one with a small scratch in the wood, and quietly uttered the questions she had saved for God alone.

Did I miss something? Or is this the plan?

Her calling had never been in doubt and the day God called her to ministry had been like fresh air after a storm. She had stepped through the open doors with boldness, teaching, preaching, mentoring, and shepherding.
And she flourished.

But some evenings, particularly after baby dedications or Christmas dinners with friends whose cards showcase their growing families, are marked by unanswered longings and desires.

A gentle sorrow, not for what she had lost, but for what had never been.

She remembered the feeling of driving home after officiating a wedding five years earlier. The bride and groom had left in a cascade of confetti, laughing and holding hands. When it was over, Evelyn sat in her parked car and let her forehead touch the steering wheel. "Lord," she had whispered, "was there ever a version of my story where someone waited at home for me too?" She did not cry. She simply let the silence answer.

Over the years, she had encountered good men and near misses:

1. A classmate who wanted a quieter, simpler life
2. A businessman who loved her heart but not her schedule
3. A missionary whose map did not include this city
4. A gentle widower who wasn't ready to love again

Each goodbye was part sorrow, part relief.

One, in particular, still stung.

A high school sweetheart named Christopher. They were twenty-one when he proposed the idea of marriage. But when Evelyn shared her calling to preach, he looked at her with gentle sadness and said, "I love you, but I need someone who wants to build a life around home, not a pulpit." The goodbye had been mutual, but it felt like losing a future she had once imagined.

She had not chosen ministry over love.
She had chosen obedience amid uncertainty.

On a gray Thursday in February, her assistant forwarded an email with the exclamation, "This gig sounds perfect for you!"

A regional women's leadership conference invited Evelyn to speak on the theme:

"The Gift of Becoming"
Our journeys shape our contributions to leadership and community.

Her first instinct was to decline. Preaching Scripture was easy. But sharing the tender, unfilled spaces of her story felt like setting a fragile vase on a table crowded with people carrying diaper bags and wearing wedding rings.

What would she tell them?
Was her single status a warning?
Or... a witness?

A thread of faith ran through the complicated terrain of her life. She knew experience makes preaching powerful, but she questioned whether hers was enough.

She often sat with these questions late at night, especially on birthdays or holidays. She would fix a cup of tea, sit in her favorite chair by the window, and whisper, "lord, I trust you... But some days, I don't know what to do with this empty space." And just as quietly, a peace would settle, not as answers, but as a presence.

She wondered:

1. How could she teach about marriage when she had never worn a ring?
2. How could she speak of motherhood without ever rocking a child to sleep?

3. Would her voice sound hollow?
4. Would her story be dismissed?

F'or many, these would be reasons to shrink back. But Evelyn had learned something sacred:

She had learned that love does not live only in marriage. She had held the hands of dying saints, wiped tears from teenagers who saw her as family, and stood in gaps for single mothers and widowed fathers. God had given her a different kind of family, not through blood, but through calling.

Waiting hadn't made her weak.
It had made her deep.

She stood in her truth without apology.
And in doing so, she gave countless others, especially those overlooked, unseen, or delayed, permission to stand in theirs.

That evening, she called Margaret her dear friend, truth-teller, and director of a Chicago nonprofit. Margaret had survived divorce and found a brave second life. They swapped updates easily, as always.

Finally, Evelyn read the speaking invitation aloud.

"What's the tightness in your chest saying?" Margaret asked.

"That I'm not a good example of becoming," Evelyn admitted with a half-laugh. "I could teach a breakout on waiting without knowing."

"You already taught me that," Margaret said softly. "When my marriage ended, you told me God's love wasn't smaller because of my disappointment. Evelyn, your story isn't a consolation prize. It's a different kind of victory."

Tears stung Evelyn's eyes. Margaret had always had a way of stripping lies from a wound. And hearing someone call her life a "victory" made her heart quietly tremble as if God was amen-ing through a friend.

After they hung up, Evelyn sat in her living room surrounded by photos:

1. Baptisms
2. Youth retreats
3. Mission trips
4. Spiritual daughters and sons

Her walls were complete.
Her life was complete.

She opened her laptop and typed, "I would be honored to speak.

The conference hall in Birmingham buzzed with nerves, coffee, and quiet hope. Three hundred women filled the room: executives, educators, mothers, widows, students, divorcees, and those still discerning their path.

Backstage, Carmen, the organizer, squeezed Evelyn's hands.

"We don't need another polished testimony," she said. "We need someone to tell the truth."

Evelyn's heart skipped a beat at what she said. She was unaware of the extent of her expectations for flawless performance. To polish her suffering, to conceal her pain. But God was only asking for her presence, not perfection.

Evelyn stepped onto the stage.
Her notes felt like prayer in her hands.

"My name is Evelyn Ross," she began.

"I have never been married. I do not have biological children."

A murmur swept through the room afterwards, followed by a peaceful silence.

"And," she continued with a gentle smile,
"I have lived a beautiful life."

She let the sentence linger.
It rested on the crowd, like truth finally relieved of its burden.

"I used to think I missed life with anniversaries and PTAs," she said.
"I wondered if my calling cost me a family.
But here is what I've learned:
I did not miss something.
I was entrusted with something."

She spoke of the sacred margins of her work:

1. Babies she baptized
2. Couples she counseled
3. Saints she buried
4. The teens she discipled
5. Nights she spent at hospitals
6. Mornings, she spent in quiet prayer

She described the beauty of availability:

1. Saying yes to late-night emergencies
2. Holding space for others' battles
3. Being present when someone needed a listening ear

Then she shared a story she had never told publicly about a teenage girl named Bria, who had shown up at her office one night, sobbing about a broken home and a broken heart. "You are the only mom I've ever known who doesn't leave," Bria had said. Evelyn paused on stage, letting the memory breathe. "In that moment," she told the audience, "I realized God had given me children, not through birth."

She closed with:

"Waiting well is not waiting perfectly.
It is living fully while you wait, trusting God's timing for what happens, what doesn't, and what happens later."

The room softened.
Faces shone.
Tears fell freely.

A steady, sacred silence filled the air.

Afterward:

A nonprofit director said she had treated her career like a placeholder for a "real life."

A widow whispered, "I thought my purpose died with my husband."

A college student said, "I thought singleness meant something was wrong with me. You helped me see it differently."

Even a little girl approached her, clutching her mother's hand, and said, "You sound like God was talking through you." Evelyn's heart nearly gave out from the kindness of it.

Later in her hotel room, she kicked off her heels and stared out at the glowing city lights.

She texted Margaret:
It wasn't a disaster. It felt like church.

Margaret replied, Of course it did. You told the truth.

Evelyn opened her journal.

Thank you for entrusting me with this exact life.
For the ache that keeps me human
And the work that makes me whole.
Teach me to wait bravely, not as someone who pretends, but as someone who believes goodness is already here.

Peace washed over her.
She was not finished.
She was not fixed.
But she was steady.

The waiting was going well.

And for the first time in a long time, Evelyn gently uttered a prayer not of petition but of praise: "Thank you for loving me in the in-between."

Reflection Questions

1. Where are you in a "hallway between doors"?
2. What have you assumed you "missed" that might actually be an entrustment?
3. How can you practice availability this week without resentment?
4. What honest sentence could you say to God tonight without performance?

Scriptures for Reflection

Psalm 27:14
"Wait for the Lord; be strong and take heart and wait for the Lord."

Isaiah 40:31
"But those who hope in the Lord will renew their strength. They will soar on wings like eagles; they will run and not grow weary; they will walk and not be faint."

Lamentations 3:25–26
"The Lord is good to those whose hope is in him, to the one who seeks him; it is good to wait quietly for the salvation of the Lord."

Proverbs 3:5–6
"Trust in the Lord with all your heart and lean not on your own understanding; in all your ways submit to him, and he will make your paths straight."

7

LOVE WITHOUT LIMITS

Serving Beyond Boundaries

Isaiah 6:8 (NIV)
"Here am I. Send me!"

Leah Thompson believed in clarity—color-coded calendars, laminated checklists, and meetings that started and ended precisely on time. For six years, she had led volunteer efforts at Grace Commons with military precision, turning chaos into order and noble intentions into transformative service.

Her husband, Caleb, an art teacher who found beauty in broken things, balanced her in ways she never asked for but desperately needed. Their apartment walls told their story: his watercolor paintings of puddle-splashed children, elderly hands in prayer, and sunlight streaming through cracked windows. Where Leah saw problems to solve, Caleb saw stories to honor.

But lately, something in their rhythm had shifted; not conflict, but calling.

This event occurred on a Thursday in late November. Caleb left the house to complete a twenty-minute errand and returned three hours later, face pale with the kind of overwhelmed artists get when their soul has collided with something more profound than words.

"I made a mistake," he said softly. "I took a wrong turn... through East Hollow."

Leah froze.

East Hollow was twenty minutes away but a world apart. The scene shifted from aging apartments and boarded-up shops to children playing in cracked parking lots, while elderly residents pushed broken carts because buses were unreliable.

"And do you know what I didn't see?" Caleb's voice dropped. "Not a single church. Not one."

Leah swallowed. "Are you saying... we should do something about that?"
Her voice was barely above a whisper, because the truth was she had been wrestling with that same question for months, but fear kept her from saying it aloud.

A thought she had managed to avoid for years rose up again: what if God was calling her to something that didn't fit on a checklist? This time, she didn't push it down. She let it sit, let it stretch her, and let it scare her.

Caleb nodded. "Yes. But... not a program. It's not an initiative but something tangible. Something *real*."

Leah blinked. "What do you mean, real?"

He paused, searching for words.
"A place where people don't have to perform," he said quietly.
"A place where faith lives in kitchens and backyards. A place where people are seen."

A house church.

The word landed in Leah's chest like a drumbeat: steady, wild, and terrifying. She had spent years building ordered systems, structures, and safety nets. A house church was none of those things. It was raw, human, and unpredictable, which made something in her spirit flare up.

"Real," she repeated.
"Not about filling seats… but filling lives."

Caleb nodded again, slower this time, as if letting the idea settle between them like fresh soil waiting for seeds.

Leah took a long breath, her mind racing.
She had always believed big problems needed big solutions, well-built programs, strategic plans, and flawless execution.

But now, a different question surfaced:

What if God was asking for something small? What if just small was holy?

A house church meant:

1. No flyers
2. No schedules
3. No tight agendas
4. No rows of chairs
5. No "success metrics."

Just presence.
Just people.
Just love.

"Let's start small," she whispered.
"Invite a few people. No pressure. No performance. Just… love."

Caleb smiled softly.
"Exactly."

And yet, the weight of it settled on her shoulders, not heavy, but sacred.

She had always been afraid of failing in public. But this time, God was asking her to risk failing in private, which felt even more intimate.

After weeks of praying, journaling, fasting, and wrestling, the breakthrough came unexpectedly.

At a women's gathering, Pastor Evelyn said, "There are times when obedience feels like letting go of comfort."

The words hit Leah so hard that she actually stopped breathing for a moment. It was as if God had been waiting for her to hear that sentence. And finally, she was ready.

That night, in the dark, she spoke quietly,
"Let's go to East Hollow."

Caleb's smile was audible in the quiet room.

"Are you sure?"

"No," she admitted.
"But I'm sure God is bigger than my fear. And maybe that's enough."

Their first connection was Mrs. Dorothy Hargrove, age 68, who had lived in East Hollow for forty years. She welcomed them with cinnamon rolls and cautious eyes.

"What we need," she said plainly, "are people who show up and stay."

Then she surprised them.

"You can use my backyard. That old oak tree still gives good shade. The fence needs fixing anyway."

Leah felt her heart break and heal at the same time. Here they were showing up with a vision, and God was sending them a woman who had been praying for years without telling anyone.

On the first Thursday of January, twenty-three people gathered under the oak tree behind Dorothy's house.

String lights, Caleb hung, fluttering in the winter breeze.
James repaired the fence.
Jacob facilitated a devotional.
Zara read Scripture.
Eli arranged chairs and poured coffee.
Micah passed out song sheets as if it were his life's mission.

A dog barked.
Kids ran around.
A skeptical teen with purple hair sat cross-armed in the corner.

And Leah?

She breathed.

For the first time in years, she prayed without trying to control the outcome. She let her heart be a participant instead of a leader. She let the Holy Spirit set the agenda. And it felt like freedom.

It wasn't polished.
It wasn't perfect.
But it was real.

And that was enough.

In the weeks that followed, East Hollow bloomed.

1. Alex, the skeptical teen, brought two friends.
2. Dorothy's neighbor, Teresa, opened her apartment for young moms.
3. James launched "Fix-It Fridays" to restore dignity through repair.
4. Jacob started a writing group that turned pain into poetry.
5. Zara formed a single-parent support circle.
6. Eli hosted youth basketball nights in an old parking lot.

And Leah?

She changed.

She stopped tracking attendance.
She let go of her obsession with structure.
Stopped measuring success by numbers.
She started listening. She started resting.
She started seeing people and letting them see her, too.

She learned that success wasn't something you count.
It was something you witnessed.

Lives transforming.
Hearts softening.
Hope reviving.
Roots deepening.

One March evening, beneath blooming window boxes and cool spring air, Leah felt something shift inside her.

She wasn't leading a ministry.
She was part of a movement.

Love without limits.

It wasn't a flashy program.
It wasn't a growth strategy.

It was the kingdom right there under an old oak tree in a forgotten neighborhood.

On the drive home, she squeezed Caleb's hand.

"Thank you for seeing what I couldn't," she whispered.

He kissed her forehead.
"That's what love is," he murmured.
"Taking turns being brave."

And in that moment, Leah realized something holy: God hadn't called her to build a big ministry, but instead, he had called her to love big.

Some nights she cried quietly, thinking:

What if this fails? What if people don't believe in the vision? What if we're wrong?

But the louder truth was one she couldn't ignore:

What if this was exactly what God was waiting for: two people willing to serve without limits or labels?

She remembered a line she once read from Rick Warren:

"The purpose of your life is far greater than your own personal fulfillment."
And for the first time, she believed it with her whole heart.

"Let's keep going," she whispered.

This was only the beginning of love without limits.

Reflection Questions

1. What comforts are you clinging to that might keep you from obedience?
2. Where is God calling you beyond your comfort zone?
3. What small act of faith could make a bigger impact than you realize?
4. What does "love without limits" look like for you this week?

Scriptures for Reflection

Isaiah 6:8,

"Then I heard the voice of the Lord saying, 'Whom shall I send? And who will go for us?' And I said, 'Here am I. Send me!

Matthew 25:40

"The King will reply, 'Truly I tell you, whatever you did for one of the least of these brothers and sisters of mine, you did for me.'"

2 Corinthians 12:9,

"But he said to me, 'My grace is sufficient for you, for my power is made perfect in weakness.' Therefore, I will boast all the more gladly of my weaknesses, so that the power of Christ may rest upon me."

James 2:17

"In the same way, faith by itself, if it is not accompanied by action, is dead."

8
THE QUIET HERO

Greatness in the Shadows

Matthew 6:4 (NIV)
"Your Father, who sees what is done in secret, will reward you."

Lydia Hartman had spent her entire life serving in the background in various capacities, such as cleaning communion trays, rocking babies, and showing up with warm casseroles when words were insufficient. It had been five years since Frank had gone to be with Jesus, and the house had settled into a silence that sometimes felt like fog around it. The mornings consisted of a single cup of coffee rather than two. It was now time for her son Jacob to have his space and his rhythm. She continued to perform faithful actions such as unlocking doors at Grace Commons on Sundays, straightening pews, and refilling prayer cards. These repetitive actions did not require the use of microphones or spotlights.

Am I still required?

Am I still needed?

This is a common question that people ask when things do not seem to be going as planned. Nevertheless, God has wonderful things in store for his children.

On a Thursday Community Outreach Night, Lydia arrived to handle registration, only to find eager college volunteers already running the table. She hovered, tote bag in hand, suddenly unsure where to fit. Outside, near the new community garden, a young mom wrestled a crying toddler while three children zigzagged dangerously close to the beds James had helped build.

Instead of thinking, Lydia moved her body. Knees protesting, she knelt to the children's eye level and opened her well-worn tote, which contained crayons, small coloring books, animal crackers, and wet wipes. She inquired, "Would you like to color with me?" They gathered under the old magnolia, petal-soft and trusting. As tiny hands filled paper with farm animals and flowers, Lydia hummed 'Jesus Loves Me,' then 'Amazing Grace.' A pigtailed girl climbed into her lap. "I like your voice," she whispered. "It's God's voice when I sing," Lydia answered, surprised by the truth of it.

A passing volunteer snapped a photo: Lydia in a circle of children, chaos calmed by gentleness. She posted it on the church board with the caption, "This wonderful woman made my kids feel safe and loved. Thank you for demonstrating this kind of ministry to us. The post had received hundreds of likes and dozens of comments by Sunday, naming grandmothers, nursery workers, and "church ladies" who had loved them into faith.

This indicates that the post had significantly spread beyond the confines of the church.

After the service, Pastor Evelyn found Lydia collecting bulletins. "Your presence changed that night," she said warmly. "Would you consider writing short reflections?

We will refer to them as "Porch Devotion: wisdom shared like sweet tea on a front porch." Lydia hesitated. "Pastor, I'm no theologian. I'm... steady." Evelyn pressed a small notebook into her hands. "Steadiness is theology we can touch."

Lydia stared at the blank page while sitting at her kitchen table, which had previously served as a place for her to complete her homework and pray in the evening. Daffodils were growing through the soil she had previously believed was dead. She wrote that even dry ground can blossom when it is loved. When we planted these bulbs many years ago, we lost track of them. Without a doubt, they rose today. Perhaps grace operates in this manner: unseen at first, then suddenly revealed. The faithfulness of God is not contingent on my memory; instead, it continues to increase.

The post traveled, reaching young mothers, widows, caregivers, and those who were exhausted. It received 400 shares in a span of days. A week later, a spring storm blew in. Lydia watched from her covered porch and wrote: The wind doesn't ask permission. It rearranges everything. Faith doesn't stop the wind; it trusts the shelter. That one went viral, and emails began to arrive: "I thought my quiet life didn't count." "I'm caring for my mother; your words helped me breathe." Jacob helped her sort the messages, smiling at the wonder of it.

One Sunday, Jacob sank into Frank's recliner with a glass of sweet tea. "You know you're internet famous, right?" he teased. Lydia greeted him with a wave, but he became more serious. Your post, which read, "Don't mistake quietness for absence," had a significant impact on me. When my father passed away, I made an effort to be loud and strong. You were consistent and powerful. I came dangerously close to missing it." Gentle and appreciative tears began to fall. According to her, "God provided us both with what we required." It's just that we haven't seen it yet.

By May, the women's ministry asked Lydia to speak at their spring brunch. Public speaking wasn't her lane, but the porch had taught her courage. She stood before seventy-five women, ranging from college students to octogenarians, her hands shaking, her voice steady. As she started, she introduced herself by saying, "I am a widow, a mother, a gardener, and apparently a devotional writer." "I am someone who, for the most part, pondered whether or not her quiet life still mattered." According to her, consistency is more important than charisma, casseroles are more important than platforms, and the kingdom is built by those who never get plaques.

When she finished, the room responded with a prolonged, tear-filled ovation, a gesture that conveys the message that we recognize you.

That evening, Lydia sat on her porch, the soft scent of chamomile drifting from her teacup, cooling slowly in the fading light of dusk. Her journal was open, the pages waiting to hold her thoughts like they always did, a quiet ritual she had come to treasure.

The neighborhood around her began to shift as the evening unfolded: lights flickered on one by one in the windows of nearby homes, a gentle glow spilling out to meet the encroaching darkness. Children's voices echoed through the air, laughter and calls to come inside, their footsteps thudding lightly on the sidewalk as the sun dipped lower.

Lydia's pen hovered over the page, and then she began to write words flowing from her heart, a quiet prayer whispered into the night.

She wrote, "Lord, thank You for letting my small life speak," and the ink flowed like a prayer of surrender as she completed the sentence. She took a momentary pause, her gaze wandering over the peaceful neighborhood, which, despite the presence of familiar faces and lives lived in close proximity, remained so distinct and individual.

What was my life in the grand story? she wondered. What could it possibly mean in the vast expanse of the world?

But the answer came gently. It was enough. She could feel it in her bones, in the rhythm of her breath, and in the stillness of the evening. If my lap can be a sanctuary and my words a shelter, keep me faithful. It was a quiet prayer of service, of living faithfully in the small spaces she had been given. The world often clamored for grand gestures, for accolades, for the shining spotlight. On the other hand, Lydia believed deep down that she was destined for something less complicated and more peaceful.

She took a moment to close her eyes and centered her thoughts on the people she had met throughout her life, including friends, neighbors, and even strangers who had come through her life.

How many had walked through my door, seeking refuge in a cup of tea or a listening ear? she thought. How many had left with a little more peace than they arrived with?

Not every individual required the spotlight. It was not necessary for everyone to have their name displayed on a marquee or to stand before large crowds. Some people were tasked with the role of the unsung heroes, the individuals who performed their duties in the background, providing a simple presence and a steady hand. Lydia realized that she was like a lamp on a porch, glowing softly in the night. It was not a fire, but it was sufficient to lead weary feet back to their destination, to provide warmth, and to assist in finding direction when the path appeared uncertain.

Her role was not to be loud but to be steady and faithful to the little things. In the gentleness of a quiet evening spent in prayer, the moments she gave to others and the way she lived her life with open hands were enough.

This sacrifice was her offering. She didn't need the world to know her name or see her every act of kindness. What mattered was that in the quiet moments, in the subtle, unnoticed gestures, she was fulfilling the work she was called to do.

Lydia set the pen down; her heart settled with a deep peace. She didn't need the world's applause. She only needed to be faithful to her heart's calling.

And in the stillness of that moment, she knew it was enough.

After putting the journal away, she took a sip of her chamomile tea and looked out at the neighborhood, which she considered her personal, peaceful enclave in the world. A lamp on a porch, brightly shining in the darkness, illuminating the path for weary feet to return home.

Reflective Questions

1. Where have you believed your quiet contributions don't count? What small act of faithfulness can you offer this week?

2. Who taught you the power of steady love? How can you thank or imitate them now?

3. What "porch devotion" could you write? One paragraph of lived wisdom to share with someone weary?

4. How might God be inviting you to make a safe place for children, caregivers, or the overlooked?

Scripture for Reflection

Matthew 6:4
"Your Father, who sees what is done in secret, will reward you."

Proverbs 31:26
"She opens her mouth with wisdom, and the teaching of kindness is on her tongue."

1 Thessalonians 4:11
"Make it your ambition to lead a quiet life."

Galatians 6:9
"Let us not grow weary in doing good... at the proper time we will reap a harvest."

9

WHEN DREAMS WAKE UP

Season of Restoration

Joel 2:25 (NIV)

"I will restore to you the years the locusts have eaten."

Elias Montgomery had once led with fire, passionately and with enormous intensity. For twenty-three years, he pastored growing churches across Georgia and Alabama, his voice carrying a conviction born of love.

June, his wife, played piano like a prayer; their son Benjamin clapped along from the front pew. Sundays blurred into potlucks and late-night prayer meetings. Elias believed God could do anything until the day God didn't.

The call came on an October Tuesday, which was just another day in Elias's regular routine. Early in the afternoon, there was the usual buzz of routine: coffee in the morning, meetings, and the regular office work at church. But that call, that sudden break, would change the way he spent the rest of his days forever.

A drunk driver. A red light that was missed. June, his wife, and their 25-year-old son, Benjamin, were gone in an instant.

At first, the police officer's words on the phone sounded like a faraway echo, as if they were meant for someone else. An unknown voice said, "There was an accident at the intersection."

I'm truly sorry, sir. Unfortunately, your wife and son did not make it through."

Elias' knees gave way, and the phone fell from his hand and landed on the floor with a grave sound. He could only hear the dull sound of his breathing. It was like the world had turned on its axis. His chest was beating fast, with each beat being louder than the last. This was his mind trying to catch up with what his body already knew to be true. They were no longer there. The world had taken them away in the blink of an eye.

Thereafter, the days went by quickly. The shock went away, but the numbness persisted, making it difficult to breathe. He was so shocked that he couldn't believe his life had changed into something he didn't recognize. Elias went through the steps like a ghost while the funeral plans were being made. He took care of the details, planned the service, and said the things he needed to say. But it all felt like a show for nothing. He was in so much pain that it felt like it could swallow him whole.

How could he be sad?

The service at the gravesite took place on a cloudy, gray morning. The air was heavy with sadness, and the cold breeze carried the smell of freshly turned soil. A small group of twelve people who knew June and Benjamin from church, family, and other social groups was there. But Elias felt like they were all strangers because he was watching from afar as the Georgia clay ate up the bodies of his wife and son.

Elias felt a deep sense of despair with each shovel of dirt that fell. As he stood there, he didn't say a word. He could feel the earth's weight pressing against his chest. It was difficult to hear the pastor's words of comfort because they were so far away. He could only hear the noise of his thoughts, which kept going around and around in his head.

As the last words were said, Elias knew that everything was over. His family, his whole world, was dead and buried in front of him. And along with them, something profound and vital in his spirit felt buried.

The following Sunday, Elias stood at the podium, feeling like the whole world was pressing down on him. As every Sunday, the church was full of people eager for the comfort of Bible readings and teachings. But for Elias, it was all strange. He couldn't feel good and loving in his heart, so how could he tell these people that God was good and loving? How could he praise the constancy of a God who let such terrible things happen? The words were laborious for him to say because his chest hurt so much.

He looked at everyone in the church, and every face made him think of what he had lost. He tried to talk to them and give them some of the hope he had once carried so easily. It seemed like a lie, though. His words were empty, like vestiges of a religion he no longer had. The congregation heard, but they had no idea how upset he was inside. Their eyes were on him, but he felt like he was a million miles away, cut off from them by a chasm of sadness and doubt that no one could cross.

After the service that Sunday, Elias did something he never thought he would do. Along the edge of the platform, he put his hands and looked out at the sea of faces. Each one was waiting for something he no longer had to give. Every word he said was saturated with the pain he could no longer hide. His voice was quiet but firm.

He told her, "I can no longer speak of God's goodness." The weight of his confession made his voice break. "When I cannot feel it myself."

Even though it was only one phrase, it felt like a statement or the end of a chapter. It was difficult to breathe in the room, the shock and understanding filling the silence. He didn't try to make excuses or explain how he felt. He just resigned from his job as a pastor, the thing that made him who he was, and left the church he had led with unshaken belief.

Elias felt free for the first time in years. He felt lighter without the weight he had been carrying. He had no more tasks to carry out or sermons to preach. There was only the quiet, painful truth of his grief and the unspoken admission that even for religious people, there are times when the soul can't make sense of the pain it goes through.

After that, Elias pulled away from the life he had known and went to the quiet places in his heart where he could no longer lie. He walked for hours and thought. In a way, he was mourning not only his family but also the old version of himself that had died with them. Though he would eventually return to his faith, he needed to feel his pain right now. He needed to let it be a part of him as he found his way back to God, not as a priest but as a broken man looking for healing.

At that very moment, when Elias was about to give up, he gained a new understanding of something that preachers were unable to convey. A deeper understanding of what it means to grieve profoundly, to lose someone without any prior warning, and to possess the resilience to be open and vulnerable even after the most devastating loss. Even though he had no idea what the future was going to bring, he was aware that he did not have to pretend to be anything. He returned empty and not in a perfect state.

Mr. Elias, the quiet widower who arrived early, folded chairs, locked doors, and prayed over empty pews, moved to Grace Commons and sat in the back row. He moved three states away and concealed himself there.

For five years he lived by routine: coffee at five, volunteering by eight, errands, evening news, and early bed. He spoke when spoken to and guarded his story like a secret that might shatter if touched.

But God wasn't finished with him.

There was no doubt that God had not finished dealing with him.

It started with a question one Thursday in March. Elias was changing lightbulbs when Eli Thompson looked up at him and asked, "How do you know if you're hearing God or just scared?" The ache was immediate; Benjamin used to ask questions like that. Over coffee, Elias found words he thought he'd lost. "Faith isn't the absence of fear," he told Eli.

"It's moving forward with fear as a companion, not a master."

Coffee was consumed once a week and then twice a week. After James, Jacob became a member. Eli's sincere desire, James's practical wisdom with a hidden insecurity, and Jacob's creative heart and fear of exposure were all reminiscent of Benjamin that Elias heard in each of them. Being a mentor to them was like a balm and a blade at the same time; it was both healing and heartbreaking.

"You have something we need," Jacob said after a hard writing day. "Your faith has been tested." When Pastor Evelyn later asked Elias to write short devotionals for the church site, he laughed softly. "I'm hardly fit to guide anyone." "On the contrary," she said. "You've been guiding them for months."

On that particular evening, Elias penned a single paragraph while sitting at his kitchen table, where he had eaten by himself and read the Bible without feeling anything.

Sometimes the seed still grows in the field you abandoned. I walked away from ministry seven years ago, convinced my season of usefulness was over. But watching young people wrestle with faith and calling has reminded me that God's work doesn't stop when our hearts break. It just takes new forms, grows in unexpected soil, and bears fruit we never planned to harvest.

It was sent by him. Over one thousand people had shared it by the time Sunday rolled around. A series of brief, truthful, and consistent reflections followed. People began asking, Who is this Mr. Elias? The truth: a broken minister learning to trust God again through the faith of the young.

He realized that the years of silence were not a form of penance but rather preparation. To reconstruct what the accident had shattered, each chair was folded, the floor was swept, and each conversation was repeated. A sense of hope returned, not naive but profound.

Then came the stroke, on a Wednesday in November while setting up for the Thanksgiving event. His left side seized; words tangled. Jacob found him, then James, then Eli. In the ER waiting room, Jacob remembered a sealed envelope tucked in Elias's open Bible: To be read whether I make it or not.

Elizabeth, James, Jacob, Pastor Evelyn, Leah and Caleb, Lydia, and Jacob gathered together, and Jacob read the following:

My dear friends,

If you are reading this, it means that either my stubborn heart has given out or God is reminding us that none of us is guaranteed tomorrow. Seven years ago, I buried my calling with my family. I came here to fade away. However, you, Eli, James, and Jacob, revived my dreams that I had buried. Through your questions and trust, you made me believe again not only in God's goodness but also that broken things are useful in His hands.

I thought ministry meant answers. You taught me that ministry involves walking alongside those who are brave enough to ask questions. I thought influence required a platform. You showed me that influence occurs in coffee shops and hallways where people connect with one another. My Benjamin would be your age now.

Being a mentor to you has been like falling in love with him once more, not as a replacement, but as a gift.

Pain is not wasted. These silent years were preparation. If I don't make it back, know this: you are ready. You don't need my permission to step into what God is calling you toward. If I do, then God still has work for this old minister to do.

With gratitude for resurrection,

Elias Montgomery

P.S. My real name is Dr. Elias Montgomery. I used to pastor churches. Now I'm learning that ministry is wherever love shows up to do the work.

In a gradual manner, Elias regained his speech, and his movement was measured in inches. At the same time, however, something more stable came back: the conviction that God not only resurrects bodies but also dreams.

Three months later, in Mrs. Hargrove's backyard, Elias faced a circle of neighbors under the oak. His voice was gentler, his steps deliberate, but his eyes were bright. "I used to think legacy ended with loss," he said. "That when my family died, my calling died too. I was wrong. Legacy is what survives the storm. It's what grows in gardens we thought were dead. It's when our pain becomes someone else's hope."

'Legacy is what survives the storm.'

He gestured towards the lives that were in front of him, including Eli with Zara and Micah; James, whose Build Brothers employees had increased to six; and Jacob, whose words inspired others to take courage. One of his statements was, "They didn't just wake up my dreams." Because of them, I learned that dreams are not about what we accomplish; rather, they are about what we leave behind.

People stood up, not for the purpose of putting on a show, but rather in acknowledgement of the truth. Laughing, Elias sat down. For the first time in seven years, he experienced a fully alive feeling. This was not because the pain had disappeared; rather, it was because it was a part of a larger narrative.

Dreams hadn't died; they had waited for spring.

And sometimes, if we're very fortunate, we live to see them bear fruit in those we love.

The true test of life comes not in the moments of ease or comfort, but when we are faced with the very real possibility of losing everything we hold dear or the things that have shaped our identity, our purpose, and our sense of security. It's in those moments, when the earth beneath us trembles and the very foundations of our life are shaken, that we are forced to reckon with our deepest fears and our most painful losses. Like Elias, we are brought face-to-face with the question:

Can I still stand? Can I still serve? Can I still love, even in the midst of the deepest sorrow?

For Elias, the loss of his wife, June, and his son, Benjamin, was not just the end of a chapter; it was the shattering of the life he had known. The grief that consumed him felt unbearable, and for a while, the weight of that loss threatened to extinguish the very passion that had once burned so brightly within him. How could he continue in service when his heart felt so barren and broken, despite being a man who had dedicated his life to preaching about the goodness of God? How could he speak of God's love when he could no longer feel it himself?

Nevertheless, the true test of life is not whether we falter in the face of our losses. The question is whether, in the wake of hopelessness, we are still able to muster the bravery to serve. It's the quiet, steadfast vow to continue moving forward, even when the road ahead is uncertain, even when the pain feels unbearable. For Elias, the act of walking away from the pulpit was not a surrender but a recognition of his humanity, a stepping aside to grieve and heal in his time, knowing that true service begins in the raw, unfiltered honesty of one's brokenness.

Those who survive the deepest trials, those who find the strength to rise after their world has crumbled, are the true heroes. They are true heroes not because they lack scars, but because they choose to persevere in spite of them. They are the ones who can look back at the darkness and say,

I have been there, and yet I will move forward.

They carry their stories of pain and redemption with humility, knowing that their journey can help others who are having trouble finding their way. Like Elias, these survivors not only survive for themselves but also strive to inspire future generations by demonstrating that there is always a path out of adversity.

In the kingdom of God, true service is not measured by titles, accomplishments, or outward success. It is measured by the willingness to serve with a heart full of both joy and sorrow, with hands that have been broken and mended again. The kingdom's heroes, like Elias, choose to continue serving despite the pain.

They become the ones who point the way for others, who offer a hand to those who are lost, and who remind us that it is in our brokenness that God's grace is most clearly seen. Their stories of perseverance and faith inspire those who will follow, encouraging them to keep moving forward with passion and purpose, even when the path seems impossible.

For those of us who walk in the footsteps of these heroes, we are reminded that service is not about perfection; it is about the willingness to keep going, to keep giving, even when we are tempted to withdraw into our pain. It's about choosing to love and serve others, not because we have it all together, but because we know the power of grace in the midst of our imperfections.

Consequently, those individuals who are able to endure the trials of life, such as Elias, become the very foundation upon which the work of the kingdom is built.

They are the ones who illuminate the path for future generations, demonstrating that, despite the profound darkness, the radiance of service remains constant.

Reflective Questions

1. What part of your story have you treated as disqualification rather than preparation?

2. Who might God be inviting you to mentor? What first step could you take this week?

3. What dream is asleep beneath grief or fear—and what small action could wake it?

4. How can your testimony become someone else's healing, safely and honestly?

Scripture for Reflection

Joel 2:25
"I will restore to you the years the locusts have eaten."

Psalm 71:18
"Do not forsake me... till I declare your power to the next generation."

Romans 11:29
"God's gifts and his call are irrevocable."

Isaiah 43:19
"See, I am doing a new thing... do you not perceive it?"

10

FULL CIRCLE, FULL HEART

Completed in Grace with a Fulfilled Soul

Philippians 1:3–6 (NIV)
"I thank my God every time I remember you... he who began a good work in you will carry it on to completion."

The fellowship hall had changed significantly over the past year since the folded prayer card and quiet plea were submitted. Eli Thompson stood there and thought it felt more like a family gathering than a church event. There were string lights hanging from the ceiling. Wildflowers from Mrs. Hargrove's yard filled up Mason jars to the brim.

Caleb wrote "Faith in Bloom: A Year of Growth" by hand on the signs that night.

This was not an event to raise money. The way in which ordinary people responded positively to extraordinary invitations and the ripples that those responses caused was reminiscent of a homecoming.

Eli opened the small black journal he'd started at that first prayer meeting. "My entry from one year ago," he said. "God, I don't know what I'm doing. Please show me where I belong." His voice carried the quiet authority of someone who knows he does.

Faces came into focus: Zara with Micah and two moms from her group; Jacob at the back with his camera, fully present; Leah and Caleb surrounded by East Hollow neighbors; Mrs. Hargrove waving from the middle row; James with three apprentices; Lydia in the back rocking a baby; Pastor Evelyn beside Mr. Elias, whose cane rested against his chair and whose smile blessed the room.

The words "God did not simply show me where I belong" were spoken by Eli. Eli demonstrated to me the community that I am a part of, and he did so by building it piece by piece through genuine conversation. The applause was warm and consistent, and it soaked in like rain that fell on a ground that was parched due to the prolonged drought.

Zara spoke next. "A year ago, I wore shame like a backpack of rocks," she said. Broken does not mean worthless; rather, it means ready for something new, which is something that this community taught me. It was her friends that she pointed to. Currently we are a family. When feelings of love are shared, they multiply.

After the event, she gave Eli a gentle prod at the refreshment table. Are you interested in beginning with a cup of coffee? "About that community that was built one conversation at a time... Not even us?" Eli wore a grin. This is only possible if I manage to bring my journal along. Laughing, she said, "Deal." I am privileged to read the entry for tonight.

Jacob took the mic, no longer the trembling barista.

He lifted a slim book, Quiet Fire.

"Three weeks ago my work was published," he said, earning cheers. "But even when no one reads, art is ministry and writing is worship. Influence isn't platform size; it's telling the truth God gives you." He tipped a nod to Mr. Elias. "Especially when a mentor's letter wakes you up."

Leah and Caleb shared a display of photographs from East Hollow: baptisms under the oak with Alex steadying friends in the water, potlucks on picnic blankets, sidewalk-chalk Bible stories, and Scripture nights where tough questions were welcome. "We believed that leadership meant having answers," Leah said. "It involves asking brave questions and embracing humble learning." Caleb added.

The kingdom is not constructed in sanctuaries; rather, it is constructed in backyards. "Church is a family!" Mrs. Hargrove yelled out as she reached her feet. The room erupted in applause of approval.

James came last with two apprentices, Marcus and David. "I thought no degree meant no credibility," James said. "Turns out credibility is showing up and caring more about their success." Marcus said, "My hands aren't just fixing houses; they're building a future." David added, "Dropping out didn't end my life. It rerouted it." James's voice thickened. "Build Brothers employs eight now and has a waiting list. But the real win is men discovering they are valuable."

Pastor Evelyn stepped forward. "You didn't know each other a year ago." You're family tonight, which shows that the church isn't falling apart; it's just being more honest. From buildings to yards. From TV shows to love lives. From showing off to being present.

The prayer room was where the night ended. The weathered wooden box stood by. Tonight's cards were not requests but expressions of gratitude.

Eli read first: Thank you for turning my broken prayer into belonging.

Zara: Thank you for proving I'm more than what I lost.

Jacob: Thank you for giving quiet words a loud purpose.

Leah: Thank you for breaking my need to control and rebuilding it as trust.

Caleb: Thank you for turning our home into a house of healing.

James: Thank you for letting me build lives, not just things.

Lydia: Thank you; that quiet faithfulness speaks loudly.

Pastor Evelyn: Thank you for every unseen sacred moment.

Mr. Elias, slower, sure: Thank you for waking my dream from its grave. Resurrection is a daily possibility.

People continued to congregate in groups, making plans to meet for coffee, exchanging phone numbers, laughing, crying, and asserting their commitment to continue attending. Eli stayed a moment longer with the box, palm resting on the lid.

Full circle. Full heart.

Elias, Leah, Pastor Evelyn Ross, and others' paths were marked by bravery in the midst of tremendous adversity, rather than flawlessness. At some point, they had all stood on the brink of despair, wondering how they could go on when everything around them appeared so shattered and their hopes and aspirations had been crushed away. Still, they made the conscious decision to show up, flaws and all, because they believed there was a bigger purpose for their suffering than their own personal shortcomings.

A once-proud preacher, Elias, stepped down from his pulpit chair one Sunday and ended his lifelong career with only one phrase.

"I can no longer speak of God's goodness when I cannot feel it myself."

After the tragic deaths of his wife and kid in an accident, he began to speak from a place of profound honesty. He could have wallowed in his sorrow, but instead he spoke up, first for himself and later for others. As he matured spiritually, he realized that perseverance through ambiguity, rather than striving for perfection, was the true test of faith.

There were times when Leah quietly gave in, too. Being a single mother might make you feel like you're always precariously balanced. She was hesitant to launch a podcast, despite its potential as a platform for story sharing and positive reinforcement. With all the flaws in her life, how could she possibly talk to anyone?

Still, she felt compelled to show up based on the honesty of her heart. Her openness to being human, discussing brokenness and hope, and her podcast's growth were more important than any kind of polished image she may have had.

Then there was Pastor Evelyn Ross, who had quietly carried the weight of leading and serving in a society where perfection was expected of everyone for a long time. There were times when her identity as a single woman serving in ministry made her question her ability to empathize with married couples, parents, and those who felt unfulfilled by society's standards. However, Evelyn also made the conscious decision to be there, not because she knew all the answers but because she understood the significance of just being there. Truthfully sharing one's situation and having faith that God might use it to impact others is frequently more healing than having all the answers, as she discovered.

Their shared desire to serve, flaws and all, is a common thread that runs through many of their experiences. It wasn't perfection that made them effective in this imperfect world, they realized; it was their readiness to show up damaged and vulnerable so that God could use them. "Let us not give up meeting together, as some are in the habit of doing, but let us encourage one another."

(Hebrews 10:25) This is an exhortation from the Bible. Gathering, whether in person or virtually through podcasts, ministries, or quiet acts of service, was crucial to the healing process for Leah, Elias, Pastor Evelyn, and others.

All three of them are filled with gratitude today: for one another, for the lives they've impacted, and for the strength to accept their fates the way they are. A successful podcast managed by Leah, who was previously a single mother, has become a lighthouse for those who are lost or lonely. Now that he has experienced loss firsthand, Elias serves as a mentor to others who are grieving, reassuring them that there is hope and meaning in the face of adversity. Pastor Evelyn, who had doubts about her role in the kingdom before, now leads with the assurance that comes from understanding that what matters most is not our flawlessness, but our genuineness and our eagerness to help others.

Their paths came together not in trying to be perfect, but in understanding that they are all part of a bigger story that accepts their weaknesses, doubts, and mistakes. This gathering is where they realized the greatness of God's grace: it is not for the flawless, but for those who are ready to participate, to provide what little they have, and to have faith that they are a part of something bigger than themselves.

They now strive to spread the good news that no one is condemned when they put their faith in Christ. They believe that the kingdom is made up of those who arrive in the midst of chaos, brave enough to move forward even when the path ahead appears unclear, not those who are flawless. Together, they make up a community of flawed individuals who shine a light on a world that may be so gloomy at times. They have become living examples of how willingness, rather than perfection, can sometimes make the most significant difference.

Their success is because they have shown up.

Reflective Questions

1. Where has God brought you full circle this year? Name the gratitude.

2. Who helped you grow, and how can you honor them?

3. What small testimony could awaken hope in someone else this week?

4. How can you create ordinary spaces where God's extraordinary presence is welcomed?

Scripture for Reflection

Philippians 1:3–6
"I thank my God every time I remember you... he who began a good work in you will carry it on to completion."

Hebrews 10:24–25
"Let us consider how we may spur one another on... not giving up meeting together."

Revelation 12:11
"They triumphed... by the word of their testimony."

Acts 2:46–47
"They broke bread... and ate together with glad and sincere hearts."

ACKNOWLEDGMENTS

Creating Where Stories Meet has been a deeply meaningful creative journey. Although the characters and events in this book are entirely fictional, they were inspired by the quiet bravery, everyday kindness, and remarkable resilience I witness in the world around me.

I am grateful for the countless moments, conversations, and glimpses of humanity that spark imagination and remind me that stories have the power to heal, encourage, and unite us.

My appreciation also extends to every reader who chooses to embrace this book. Thank you for opening your heart to these characters and allowing their journeys to intersect with your own. May the themes of courage, community, and calling resonate with you long after you close these pages.

⬙ GROUP DISCUSSION GUIDE

Use these prompts to spark conversation after each chapter.

Chapter 1

1. What line or moment resonated most with you, and why?
2. Where did you see courage, community, or calling at work?
3. What practice or next step will you carry into this week?

Chapter 2

1. What line or moment resonated most with you, and why?
2. Where did you see courage, community, or calling at work?
3. What practice or next step will you carry into this week?

Chapter 3

1. What line or moment resonated most with you, and why?
2. Where did you see courage, community, or calling at work?
3. What practice or next step will you carry into this week?

Chapter 4

1. What line or moment resonated most with you, and why?
2. Where did you see courage, community, or calling at work?
3. What practice or next step will you carry into this week?

Chapter 5

1. What line or moment resonated most with you, and why?
2. Where did you see courage, community, or calling at work?
3. What practice or next step will you carry into this week?

Chapter 6

1. What line or moment resonated most with you, and why?
2. Where did you see courage, community, or calling at work?
3. What practice or next step will you carry into this week?

Chapter 7

1. What line or moment resonated most with you, and why?
2. Where did you see courage, community, or calling at work?
3. What practice or next step will you carry into this week?

Chapter 8

1. What line or moment resonated most with you, and why?
2. Where did you see courage, community, or calling at work?
3. What practice or next step will you carry into this week?

Chapter 9

1. What line or moment resonated most with you, and why?
2. Where did you see courage, community, or calling at work?
3. What practice or next step will you carry into this week?

Chapter 10

1. What line or moment resonated most with you, and why?
2. Where did you see courage, community, or calling at work?
3. What practice or next step will you carry into this week?

ABOUT THE AUTHOR

Grace Ajayi is a writer, leader, storyteller, and ministry encourager who believes that God can use every imperfect moment to shape purpose. With more than twenty-two years of experience leading teams across multiple industries and a lifelong commitment to uplifting people, Grace's work reflects her heart for authenticity, faith, and emotional honesty.

Grace wrote Where Stories Meet out of a deep creative inspiration to explore how everyday people navigate love, faith, community, and calling. Though the stories are fictional, they are rooted in timeless truths about resilience, grace, and the beauty that emerges when we allow ourselves to be seen. Her writing combines spiritual insight with characters that readers can relate to, showing how God meets us in unexpected places.

Grace is married, and she and her family live in the Dallas–Fort Worth, Texas, area. She serves as an Associate Pastor at her local church and mentors emerging leaders, women in technology, and faith-driven professionals. Where Stories Meet is her debut inspirational book. When she's not writing, Grace enjoys travelling, spending time with family and friends, and cooking meals that bring people together.

Connect with the Author:

Email: gracetopublish@gmail.com

Instagram: @thehouseofperez

Facebook: https://www.facebook.com/grace.ajayi